Charlotte
the Sunflower
Fairy

For Yasmin Dickinson, who loves fairies!

Special thanks to Narinder Dhami

No part of this work may be reproduced, stored in a retrieval system,
or transmitted in any form or by any means, electronic, mechanical,
photocopying, recording, or otherwise, without written permission
of the publisher. For information regarding permission, write to
Rainbow Magic Limited c/o HIT Entertainment,
830 South Greenville Avenue, Allen, TX 75002-3320.

ISBN-10: 0-545-07093-7
ISBN-13: 978-0-545-07093-5

12 11 10 9 8 7 6 5 4 3 2 1   9 10 11 12 13/0

Printed in the U.S.A.

First Scholastic Printing, February 2009

Charlotte
the Sunflower
Fairy

by Daisy Meadows

SCHOLASTIC INC.

New York   Toronto   London   Auckland   Sydney

Mexico City   New Delhi   Hong Kong   Buenos Aires

The
Fairyland
Palace

Blossom
Hall

Fairy Garden

Leafley Village

Visitors' Center

I need the magic petals' powers,
To give my castle garden flowers.
I plan to use my magic well
To work against the fairies' spell.

From my wand ice magic flies,
Frosty bolts through fairy skies.
This is the crafty spell I weave
To bring the petals back to me.

Contents

Village Visit

"*Welcome to Leafley,*" Rachel Walker read out loud as she and her best friend, Kirsty Tate, stopped at the message board outside the Visitors' Center. "*Come and see our beautiful village and our early-blooming sunflowers!*"

"Isn't Leafley a wonderful name for a village?" Kirsty laughed, as she and

Rachel waited for their parents to catch up with them. The Tates and the Walkers — plus Rachel's dog, Buttons — were spending spring break together at the Blossom Hall hotel, which was close to the little village of Leafley.

"You kind of expect a place named Leafley to be full of beautiful flowers," Kirsty went on. Rachel nodded, and then looked serious. "But will the Leafley sunflowers be blooming at all, now that the Petal Fairies' magic petals are missing?" she asked. Kirsty frowned. "Good question. We haven't found Charlotte the Sunflower Fairy's petal yet!" she exclaimed.

At the beginning of their vacation, the two girls had promised to help their fairy friends find the seven magical petals. The petals were very important because their magic helped all the flowers in the human world to bloom beautifully. But mischievous Jack Frost wanted to make flowers grow in the frozen ground around his ice castle, so he had sent his naughty goblins to steal the magic petals and bring them to him. When the fairies tried to stop the goblins in their tracks, it turned into a battle of spells between Jack Frost and the fairies. Then the petals were whirled away into the human world in a cloud of pink-and-white magic. Now Rachel, Kirsty, and the Petal Fairies were trying to return all the petals to Fairyland before the goblins could get ahold of them again.

"We've already helped Tia the Tulip Fairy, Pippa the Poppy Fairy, and Louise the Lily Fairy," said Kirsty. "Maybe we'll find another petal today."

"I hope so," Rachel agreed, as their parents joined them. "Come on, girls," said Mrs. Walker, ushering them inside. "These early-blooming sunflowers are supposed to be amazing!"

As they went into the Visitors' Center, a woman wearing a green T-shirt embroidered with bright yellow sunflowers stepped forward to greet them. "Welcome to Leafley!" she said cheerfully. "My name's Laura." She handed Rachel and Kirsty each a large badge, and the girls were delighted to see that they were in the shape of a

sunflower with glittering golden petals and dark-brown, velvety centers. They quickly pinned them on.

"You've come to visit us on a very special day," Laura went on. "The judges of the Most Colorful Village Award are coming to Leafley today, and we're hoping we might win first prize! It goes to the town or village with the prettiest plants and blooming flowers."

"Has Leafley ever won an award before?" asked Kirsty.

"Never," Laura replied. "So everyone's very excited. We've even planted some extra sunflowers to impress the judges!"

"Well, you must have

a good chance of winning," said Mr. Tate with a smile. "I've heard that the Leafley sunflowers are spectacular."

Laura's face fell. "Unfortunately, most of the sunflowers haven't bloomed as early as they usually do." She sighed. "There are only a few small ones out at the moment. It's a real shame, but there's nothing we can do about it. We're hoping that the judges will still think Leafley is lovely, anyway."

Rachel and Kirsty glanced at each other. They knew exactly why the Leafley sunflowers weren't blooming. Both girls silently hoped that they would find Charlotte the Sunflower Fairy's magic petal as soon as possible.

"Is that a map of the village?" Kirsty asked curiously, pointing at the wall behind Laura.

"Yes, it shows the Sunflower Trail," Laura explained. "If you follow the glittery sunflower stickers on the map, you'll get to see all the prettiest spots in the village. The trail starts here at the Visitors' Center, and it ends here, too."

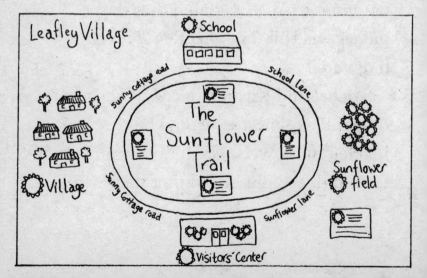

"Oh, Mom, can Rachel and I follow the Sunflower Trail, please?" Kirsty asked eagerly.

"Yes, of course," Mrs. Tate answered.

"We thought we'd have a cup of coffee before we walk around Leafley ourselves," said Mr. Walker. He pointed to the café at the back of the Visitors' Center. "So why don't you girls meet us back here in half an hour? Buttons can come with us," he added, taking the dog's leash from Rachel.

"You'll need this, girls," Laura handed Rachel a yellow envelope, sealed with a sparkly sunflower sticker. "It's a copy of the Sunflower Trail map for you to follow."

"Thank you," Kirsty and Rachel said in chorus.

The girls hurried outside, taking the envelope with them.

"Look, this is the beginning of the trail," said Kirsty, spotting a sign next to the Visitors' Center. A golden arrow pointed the way down the lane, and there was a large, glittering sunflower with a smiley face painted next to it.

"And there's the village," added Rachel.

As the girls set off along the trail, they could see the first few houses ahead of them. In front, they had neat gardens planted with sunflowers, but hardly any of them were in bloom. The buds that were flowering looked really wilted and unhappy. Their stems were flimsy and their leaves dying.

"We have to find Charlotte's magic sunflower petal!" Rachel declared. "Maybe then Leafley will have a chance to win the Most Colorful Village Award."

As she spoke, Rachel pulled the sticker off the back of the envelope that Laura had given them. Suddenly, a stream of dazzling golden sparkles burst out and swirled into the air in a glistening cloud.

"Oh!" Rachel gasped.

"It looks like fairy dust!" Kirsty exclaimed. "Quick, Rachel, see what's inside!"

Carefully, Rachel pulled the envelope open, and Charlotte the Sunflower Fairy danced out at once. The fairy gave her wand a twirl and smiled happily at the girls!

Sneaky Sunflowers

The little fairy hovered in the air. She shook out her crumpled wings and then straightened her blue pants and matching top. She had dark hair tied in bouncy bunches. Wrapped around her waist was a wide leather belt, fastened with a big, shiny sunflower buckle.

"Hello, girls!" Charlotte cried. "I'm so glad to see you."

"We thought we might find you here, Charlotte," said Kirsty. "Is there any sign of your sunflower petal yet?"

Charlotte's face fell and her wings drooped. "Not yet," she said sadly. "But I know it's in Leafley somewhere. We have to find it!"

"We can look for your petal by following the Sunflower Trail," Rachel promised, showing Charlotte the map.

"But don't forget that the goblins have a wand full of Jack Frost's icy magic to help them," Charlotte warned. "We need to be careful."

Rachel studied the map as they walked along. "This street is called Sunny Cottage Row," she announced.

There was a small group of children already on the trail ahead of them, so Charlotte hid behind Kirsty's sunflower badge. Then the girls walked toward the row of tiny cottages. The brown-and-white houses were very charming with their thatched roofs and colorful gardens of spring flowers.

But, as the girls had already noticed, hardly any of the sunflowers were in bloom. "It's a shame." Charlotte sighed, peeking out from behind Kirsty's badge. "Sunny Cottage Row is so beautiful when all the gorgeous sunflowers are out."

As they passed another pretty garden, Kirsty noticed that this one seemed to have a few more sunflowers in bloom than the others they'd seen so far. She stopped and scanned the garden carefully, searching for Charlotte's petal, but a sudden movement made her jump. Was she imagining things, or had one of the sunflowers actually twitched?

She watched it carefully for a moment, then nudged Rachel. "One of those sunflowers is moving around!" she told her friend. "First it was by the fence, but now it's over there by the shed!"

"Are you sure?" asked Rachel.

"Which sunflower was it, Kirsty?" Charlotte wanted to know.

Kirsty pointed it out.

"It's not moving now," Rachel

remarked. Then she gave a gasp. "But that one is! Look, over by the pond!"

Rachel, Kirsty, and Charlotte watched in amazement as the other sunflower ran

across the garden, petals bobbing, and stopped near the shed, too.

"That doesn't look like one of my

beautiful sunflowers," Charlotte said
doubtfully.

Rachel frowned, peering over the fence
at the flower that had moved. "No,
sunflowers don't have long, pointy
green noses," she agreed.

"That's a goblin!"

A Cold Spell

Kirsty and Charlotte looked concerned.
Now that Rachel had pointed it out,
they could see that the goblin was
wearing a headdress of yellow sunflower
petals that fit neatly around his face.

"Oh no! It's even worse than that!"
Charlotte announced, staring into the

garden at all the sunflowers. "There are lots of goblins!"

She pointed her wand at five more sunflowers, including the one Kirsty had noticed first. The girls' hearts sank as they realized that Charlotte was right. They were all goblins!

"So that's why I thought there were more sunflowers blooming in this garden

than any of the others." Kirsty groaned. "They're goblins in disguise!"

"If they hadn't moved, we wouldn't have noticed," Rachel said. "They blend in so well with their green bodies and their yellow headdresses!"

"We have to find out if the goblins have my magic petal. Right now," Charlotte declared, and she flew out

from behind Kirsty's badge. "Girls, I'm going to turn you into fairies immediately."

Rachel put down the map. She and Kirsty stood still and waited for Charlotte to shower them with magic fairy dust. One wave of Charlotte's wand, and the girls begin to shrink. Soon they had pretty, glittery fairy wings on their backs!

Charlotte, Rachel, and Kirsty zoomed into the garden where the goblins were hiding. Charlotte led the girls behind a large bush and put a finger to her lips. Then they all peeked out between the leaves.

"There's nobody on the trail now," called one of the goblins. "Quick!" He motioned to the others, losing a couple of petals from his headdress as he darted across the garden. "Start looking for the magic petal!"

The goblins immediately began a frantic search. They dashed all over the garden, roughly grabbing the sunflowers and pulling their heads down to examine the petals.

"Oh, I can't watch!" Charlotte gasped, covering her eyes with her hands. "They're ruining my poor sunflowers."

Rachel and Kirsty watched anxiously as the goblins stomped through the middle of the flower beds. *Maybe Charlotte's magic petal isn't in this garden at all,* Rachel thought doubtfully. There weren't very many sunflowers left that the goblins hadn't already examined.

Except for a clump of three plants not far from the bush where Charlotte and the girls were hiding . . .

Rachel glanced at the three sunflowers. One was much taller than the others, and its sunshine-yellow petals had opened to show the dark brown seeds in its center. *It's very strange*, Rachel thought with a frown, *but one of the petals seems more golden and sparkly than the others. . . .*

"Oh!" Rachel gasped, then clapped her hand over her mouth to stop herself from crying out too loudly. "It's the magic petal!" she whispered to her friends.

"Where?" Charlotte asked excitedly.

Rachel pointed out the tall sunflower, and Charlotte's face broke into a big, beaming smile.

"Good job, Rachel," she whispered, doing a little dance of joy in the air. "We'd better get ahold of it quickly, before the goblins do."

Charlotte whizzed out from behind the bush. Her thin, glittery wings were a blur as she raced toward her precious petal. Rachel and Kirsty followed. "Oh no you don't!" yelled a gruff voice from behind them. "That magic petal belongs to Jack Frost!"

Kirsty glanced over her shoulder to see a goblin rushing toward the sunflower. "One of the goblins has spotted us — and the magic petal!" she cried.

"Hurry, girls!" Charlotte called, her wings beating even faster.

Rachel and Kirsty flew faster than they had ever flown before as they dashed after Charlotte.

"I think we're going to get to the petal first," Kirsty panted. "The goblin's not tall enough to reach it."

But just as Charlotte and the girls arrived at the sunflower, the goblin skidded to a halt on the ground below

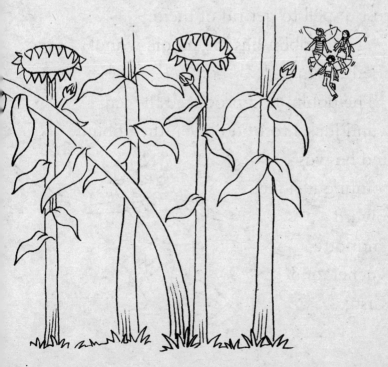

them. He grabbed the sunflower's stem
and yanked the big flower head down,
away from Charlotte and the girls.

The next moment he screeched with
triumph as he snatched the magic petal
and waved it gleefully in the air.
Charlotte, Rachel, and Kirsty looked at
each other in horror.

"I found the magic petal!" the goblin yelled to his friends, "but those pesky fairies are after me! Help!"

"Don't let them get the petal!" another goblin shouted across the garden. "I'll cast a spell to get rid of them."

"That goblin has the magic wand!" cried Kirsty.

The goblin had produced the icy wand Jack Frost had given the goblins, and he was pointing it right toward Charlotte, Rachel, and Kirsty.

"Jack Frost's freezing icy bolts will give those fairies a nasty shock!" he roared loudly.

Nothing happened.

"That's a terrible spell!" one of the other goblins yelled. "Don't you remember? It doesn't work if it doesn't rhyme!"

The goblin with the wand looked furious. "Jack Frost's freezing icy bolts will give those fairies nasty jolts!" he shouted triumphantly. "That rhymes!"

This time, the spell worked. Three sparkling ice bolts shot out from the wand and headed straight toward the three fairies.

"Look out!" yelled
Charlotte, turning
a somersault in
the air as an ice
bolt whizzed
underneath her.

Kirsty managed to
dodge the second
ice bolt, but Rachel wasn't so lucky.

The third
bolt hit her. It
instantly surrounded
her in a sheet of
ice. Rachel hovered
in the air for a second,
her face frozen in an
expression of surprise.
But then she began

to tumble toward the ground, her wings frozen solid.

"Oh no!" Kirsty cried anxiously. "She can't fly!" The goblins cackled with glee and headed out of the garden. But Kirsty flew toward her friend as she realized the awful truth. She yelled to Charlotte, "If Rachel falls to the ground, she'll shatter into icy pieces!"

Field Trip

With a flick of her wrist, Charlotte cast a fairy spell. Glittering sparkles rained from her wand onto the tall sunflower, surrounding it with magic.

As Rachel plummeted downward, the sunflower bent its golden head. It caught Rachel in its velvety brown center just as she was about to hit the ground.

Kirsty and Charlotte zoomed over to make sure Rachel wasn't hurt. She was sitting in the middle of the sunflower on a cushion of seeds, and she had the same surprised look on her face.

"She's still frozen," Kirsty said anxiously, feeling Rachel's arm. "It's like touching an icicle!"

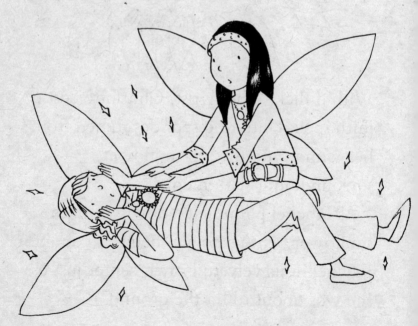

"The goblins' spells aren't as powerful as Jack Frost's magic," explained Charlotte. "The spell should wear off soon."

Kirsty took off her cardigan and wrapped it around her friend. Then she and Charlotte watched as, very gradually, Rachel began to warm up.  After a few minutes she was able to move her face, then her arms, then her legs. Soon, she was fluttering her wings and looking much happier.

"Oh, I feel better now," Rachel declared, still shivering a little. "I'm so glad I'm not a fairy popsicle anymore!

Now, where have those goblins gone with the magic petal?"

"They went further along the trail," said Kirsty, "but they couldn't have gotten very far."

As soon as Charlotte's magic had whisked the girls back to their normal size, Rachel grabbed the map and they

 all hurried off along the Sunflower Trail, searching for the goblins.

"The next stop on the trail is Leafley School," Rachel said, studying the map. "Here we are."

The girls paused outside the school to look around.

"Look at the beautiful display," said Kirsty, pointing at a huge 3-D collage that filled an entire wall of the building. The collage was made of yellow papier-mâché sunflowers and bright green cardboard leaves. The paper petals had been sprinkled with golden glitter, which made them sparkle in the sun as if they were full of fairy magic.

Rachel and Charlotte gazed at the collage in delight.

"The school's closed for spring break," said Rachel, checking to make sure that the gates were locked. "So the goblins can't be hiding in there."

They went farther along the trail, but there was still no sign of the goblins.

"We're coming up to Sunflower Field on our left," Rachel said, studying the map carefully.

"Oh, yes." Charlotte sighed. "Sunflower Field is beautiful when the sunflowers are blooming, but I don't suppose any of them will be since my petal is still missing." As the girls turned the corner of the trail, Kirsty saw a large field packed with tall, nodding sunflowers. She was expecting them all to be wilting like the others they'd seen. But to her surprise, right in the center of the field was a large circle of sunflowers in

45

full bloom, turning their golden heads cheerfully toward the sun.

"Aren't they gorgeous?" Kirsty gasped. "They're the most beautiful sunflowers we've seen all day!" Then she frowned, because the sunflowers that had looked so beautiful just a moment before were now beginning to droop in front of her very eyes!

"Ooh, look over there by the fence!" Rachel exclaimed. "There's a big patch of them, all in bloom — Oh!" Now Rachel could hardly believe her eyes. The sunflowers she'd been staring at looked as if they were dying, too!

"Over there, girls!" Charlotte cried, pointing her wand at the far end of the field. "Those sunflowers are beautiful."

"No, they're wilting now too," Rachel replied as the sunflowers Charlotte was looking at began to droop.

Charlotte looked confused. Then she twirled excitedly up into the air. "Girls, the goblins are here with the magic petal!" she announced. "They must be hiding in the field, and my petal is making the sunflowers bloom wherever they run!"

"There go the goblins!" Rachel called, pointing at another clump of blossoming sunflowers.

Kirsty burst out laughing. "The silly goblins are running around in circles!" she pointed out. Charlotte, Rachel, and Kirsty stood and watched for a few minutes as the goblins circled and zigzagged their way across the field of sunflowers. They didn't seem to have any idea where they were going.

"They could be stuck in there for

hours!" Charlotte said. "How are we going to get my petal back?"

Rachel turned to Kirsty and Charlotte, beaming. "I think I have an idea!" she declared.

Perfect Petals

Rachel gave the map to Kirsty and turned to the tiny fairy. "Charlotte, could you use your magic to make two glittery paper petals, just like the ones on the Leafley School collage?" she asked.

Charlotte laughed. "Of course I can!" she exclaimed. "Watch!"

She twirled her wand and a shower of

magic fairy dust fell
softly over Rachel.
A second later, two
large sunflower
petals instantly
appeared in one of
Rachel's hands.

"Oh, they're beautiful!" Rachel
breathed, holding them up to show
Kirsty. The petals sparkled and gleamed
in the sunshine, catching the light as
Rachel turned them this way and that.

The goblins were still rushing around
the field, clearly trying to find their way
out. They made the sunflowers bloom
and wilt everywhere they went.
Charlotte and the girls could hear
rustling noises as the goblins pushed their
way through the flower stems.

"Here goes," Rachel whispered. "Hello, goblins!" she called loudly, putting her hands behind her back. "I've got a deal for you!"

No goblins appeared, but the rustling noise suddenly stopped.

"They're listening," Kirsty whispered.

"I've got two petals," Rachel went on, keeping the petals out of sight. "And I want to swap them for your one petal!"

At that moment, a green face poked out from between the sunflower stems near the fence. A goblin was scowling at the girls.

"We're not giving you our magic petal!" he snapped. "We won't give it to anyone except

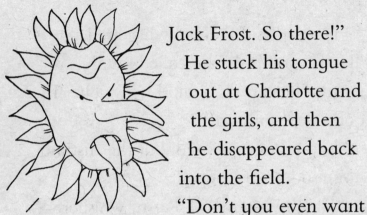

Jack Frost. So there!"
He stuck his tongue
out at Charlotte and
the girls, and then
he disappeared back
into the field.

"Don't you even want
to see my petals?" asked Rachel.
A different goblin poked his head out
suspiciously. "Let me see!" he demanded.

Rachel held up the two petals
Charlotte had given her. They looked
dazzling in the midday sun.

"Oooh!" the goblin gasped, his eyes
lighting up with greed.

"They're much bigger than your petal,
aren't they?" Rachel pointed out.

"And more sparkly!" Kirsty added.

"Hey, you!" roared the first goblin, sticking his head out again and glaring at the other one. "Don't talk to them!"

"But their petals are more sparkly," the second goblin said. "That must mean they're more magical!"

The first goblin stared hard at the petals in Rachel's hands. "Wait there!" he snapped at Rachel.

The two goblins disappeared again, and Charlotte and the girls could hear lots of whispering among the sunflowers. Rachel tried to look calm and cool, but her heart was racing. Would the goblins accept the deal?

At last the first goblin poked his head out. "We'll trade," he announced. "But only one of you can come forward with the petals. And one of us will bring our petal to you."

Rachel nodded. Immediately, one cautious-looking goblin pushed his way out of the sunflowers and came toward her. He had Charlotte's magic petal gripped tightly in his knobby green hand.

Rachel went to meet him.

"Give me one of your petals first!" the goblin demanded rudely.

Rachel held out one sparkly petal, and the goblin quickly snatched it.

Kirsty held her breath as the goblin then held out his own petal toward Rachel. The instant Rachel took it, he grabbed the other paper petal from her and danced gleefully back to his friends.

"I've got the two sparkly petals!" he boasted triumphantly.

There was a muffled cheer from inside the field and then Charlotte and the girls heard the sound of the goblins running off.

"The silly goblins have swapped the magic petal for two petals that aren't magic at all!" Kirsty giggled.

"Yes." Charlotte laughed, whizzing over to Rachel. "I'd better take my magic petal straight back to Fairyland before the goblins realize their mistake!"

Sunflower Spectacle

Charlotte flew down and gently tapped the petal sitting on Rachel's palm with her wand. It immediately shrank down to its Fairyland size.

"Thank you a thousand times, girls," Charlotte cried, picking up the tiny petal and holding it lovingly. "Enjoy the rest

of your visit to Leafley, and good luck
finding the other missing petals!"

"Good-bye, Charlotte," Kirsty and
Rachel called as the little fairy vanished
in a burst of golden magic.

"We did it, Kirsty!" Rachel beamed at
her friend. "We found another magic
petal!"

Kirsty glanced at her watch. "And we
still have some time before
we meet our parents,"
she pointed out.
"Should we keep
following the
Sunflower Trail?"

Rachel took out
the map and unfolded it.

"That's funny." She

frowned. "I don't remember seeing that before!"

Kirsty looked too and saw a small, sparkling sunflower on the map. It seemed to be marking the place on the path right next to where the girls were standing.

"Is it fairy magic?" Kirsty asked, looking thrilled.

"I think Charlotte's sunflower magic must be starting to work, now that she has her petal back," Rachel said with a

grin. "Look!" She pointed at the field. All
the sunflowers were now standing tall and
proud, turning their faces to the sun. Their
golden petals were beginning to open.

"Rachel, look at the map!" gasped
Kirsty.

The small sparkling sunflower on
the map had begun to grow a long
green stem. It curled and twisted
across the paper, following the path

of the Sunflower Trail. As Kirsty and Rachel hurried along the trail, following the stem, they noticed that sunflowers were bursting into bloom all around them. It was a delightful sight.

"All the gardens look beautiful!" Rachel said happily. "And even the sunflower decorations look like they've just been freshly painted!"

"I think every sunflower in Leafley is in bloom." Kirsty laughed.

As the girls reached the Visitors' Center, they saw a group of men and women coming out, carrying clipboards and maps of the Sunflower Trail.

"Do you think they're the judges for the Most Colorful Village award?" Rachel whispered to Kirsty.

Kirsty nodded. "It looks like Charlotte's sunflower magic has come to the rescue just in time!" she whispered back.

As the girls went inside the Visitors'

Center, they couldn't help overhearing two of the judges talking.

"I know we've seen some beautiful towns and villages while we've been judging this competition," said one of the women. "But those gardens on Sunny Cottage Road over there look absolutely spectacular! The sunflowers are beautiful."

"I know," the other judge replied. "I can't wait to see the sunflowers around the rest of the trail." She lowered her voice. "Between you and me, I think we may be looking at our winning village!"

Kirsty and Rachel looked at each other, grinning.

"Isn't petal magic amazing?" Rachel whispered. Kirsty nodded happily.

THE PETAL FAIRIES

Now Charlotte the Sunflower Fairy has
her magic petal back. Next, Rachel
and Kirsty must help

Olivia

the Orchid Fairy!

Take a look at their next adventure in
this special sneak peek!

Out and About

"Welcome to Rainbow Falls Gardens," said the man behind the desk. He picked up a garden map and counted out six tickets. Then he passed them all over the counter. "I hope you enjoy your day!"

Kirsty Tate smiled at her friend Rachel Walker as their parents thanked the man and picked up the tickets. Then the two families headed through the grand iron gates that stood at the entrance to the gardens. The Tates and the Walkers were spending spring vacation together, and so far they were having a magical time. Kirsty and Rachel hoped today would be just as exciting.

As they walked through the gates, the girls found themselves at the edge of a large grassy lawn, with a cluster of trees at the far end.

"Let's see," Mr. Walker said, opening up the map. "Where should we go first?"

Rachel, Kirsty, and Mr. Walker looked at the map. There was an orchid garden, an arboretum, and of course, the famous Rainbow Falls.

"I want to see the waterfall first," Rachel said eagerly.